CW00854881

Adventures of
Neanderthal Bob

Book 3

7 Neanderthal Bob and the Underground City

8 Bob and Siber Meet Mogar

9 Neanderthal Bob and the Winter Hunt

Stories by Keith Argyle

Illustrations by Chris Bilton

Neanderthal Bob and the Underground City

Bob walked out of his father's cave and had the feeling it would be an exciting hunting day and hoped to catch a good amount of animals to share out for everyone's evening meal.

He headed North West from the valley and hoped the weather would get brighter as the clouds were overcast and stopping the sun from shining. The weather was noticeably getting colder and soon all the main hunters of the three caves would be going on the first winter hunt together. Bob enjoyed these trips as they were able to catch bigger animals like Aurochs, large moose's and sometimes they were able to catch a woolly Mammoth.

Some of the women went with them too; their job was to cut up the animals after they had been killed.

These larger animals would keep them fed through the winter months when the snow made it difficult to hunt. They usually had two hunts for such large animals and the cave's hunters would separate into two different groups. Bob was looking forward to them happening.

As he walked down an old used track, he was wondering as always what he might catch. The path led down through the tall grass either side of it that came up to his waist. He often wondered if the grass could be used for anything other than for lying on in the caves. It was the women's job to collect it and change the old grass and straw for fresh bedding for sitting on.

He looked into the distance and could see a thick forest that was usually good for hunting smaller creatures like muskrats and the large brown rabbits. The large brown rabbits were very quick and took a lot of skill to kill them

with a sling. Bob had sometimes used his throwing spears as they were easier, but he had to get closer and that was the challenge. The large brown rabbits were very alert and could tell when people were near to them. However, Bob was a patient hunter and could wait them out and eventually kill one or two. Because of their size, he only had to catch two to be equal to three ordinary rabbits.

As he approached the forest, he looked up at the high trees. This forest had the highest trees in the area and frightened some of the other hunters as it was quite dark inside them. It didn't worry Bob about the dark, it made his senses sharper and he was always very alert when in this forest.

As he entered the thick undergrowth, he made himself ready with a throwing spear, just in case he spotted something to kill or in case something might attack him.

He didn't come here very often and didn't know any of the creatures that lived there like he

knew the squirrels in the other woodland he went to quite often.

He moved slowly and quietly being aware of any sound that was different and that could be a possible target for him to aim at. Suddenly he heard a rustling in the undergrowth and stopped dead where he was. Bob was hoping it could be a large brown rabbit. As he stood listening, he heard movement to his front right. He was sure it wasn't a large dangerous animal and thought it was going to be something he could kill easily.

Suddenly he saw the small head of a young fox. He lowered his spear and spoke to it and hoped it was friendly. He didn't kill foxes as they were too skinny and the meat wasn't very tasty.

'Hello, who are you young fox?' he asked, 'I'm Bob the Neanderthal.'

The fox looked at him a little unsure as a hunter talking to animals. 'I'm Skimpy, the fox, what are you doing in this forest?' Skimpy asked.

'I'm hunting food for my people, but I don't kill foxes, but I am able to talk to animals, especially friendly ones and those who want to be friendly with me,' Bob told him.

'Are you alone?' Skimpy asked him.

'Yes, I always hunt alone, I prefer to do it that way as I don't like following orders from others. I like to go where I want and when I want.'

'Well, Bob, I am happy to be your friend, but I must tell you that this forest is quite dangerous, large predators have been seen, even I am very careful where I go.'

'Thank you for telling me that, Skimpy, I will keep my eyes sharp and my hearing well tuned for large dangerous animals,' Bob assured him.

'Well, Bob, it's been nice making friends with you, I hope to see you again some time. I have to go, so take care and good hunting,'

Skimpy said and carried on his way and disappeared into the forest's undergrowth.

Bob waved Skimpy goodbye and carried on into the forest. He was quite thirsty and used his magic stick to ask for a drink. Within seconds, a container of cool water appeared. He drank it and the cup vanished as it had done before. He was very grateful to Julop for his magic foraging stick, he knew it was going to be a great help to him.

As he continued to walk through the trees and bushes, he thought that he saw some high rocky cliffs behind some trees. He walked closer to find that it was a long range of high rocks that were similar to the cliffs where his father's cave was.

Bob looked up and saw that the rock face was quite high; he hadn't seen high cliffs anywhere like these before, other than the cliffs where his father's caves were. He walked along them for a short distance and came to a crevice that was wide enough to walk through. Slowly

and carefully he walked through the crevice. It was about the same width all the way along about twice as wide as his body.

He suddenly stopped as he thought he could hear something further along the crevice. It sounded like voices and Morgo came to his mind, but realised that Morgo and his people lived more towards the north.

He moved slowly to where he could hear the voices better. He came to a rock that was standing in front of a large cave mouth. He peeped over it and saw some odd looking people that were dressed in strange clothing, unlike anything he had seen before.

He could see that there were men and women of what seemed to be various ages; there were even two small ones he guessed to be about five full seasons old.

One of the younger women suddenly looked over to where he was standing and he knew she had seen him. She turned and walked over to him with a friendly smile on her face.

Bob didn't feel scared as she had no weapons with her of any kind. He saw the rest of the people begin to move deeper into the cave and disappeared. The young woman walked up to the rock he was standing behind.

Bob guessed her to be about his age and stood about the same height as he was. As she came closer, she spoke to him.

'Hello, where are you from?' she asked in a warm and friendly voice.

Bob wasn't sure how to answer her. He looked at her very fair white skin that was smoother than his. He answered her, 'I'm Bob, the Neanderthal; I live South East from here,' he said to her.

She smiled and said, 'I am, Tarana, my people live deep in this cave that leads to our city. Would you like to see it?' she asked him.

Bob smiled back at her, 'I didn't know there were other people living here, I didn't even know these cliffs were here, I have never been to

this side of the forest before. But what is a city?'

Tarana looked at him closely and realised that he was from the outside world and from a very primitive people. She replied to him, 'A city is where many people live in large dwellings. Would you like to see it?' she asked him again.

'What will your people say when they see me, I might frighten them,' he said with a curious expression.

Tarana laughed at him, 'Neither you nor our people have anything to be afraid of, we are aware that there are other people who live outside our city. You will be made very welcome. My father is the leader of our people, I'm sure he would like to meet you,' she said with assurance in her voice.

'Alright then, I'll come with you if you are sure I will be acceptable. We are not aware that your people live in this underground cave. How long have you been here?'

Tarana smiled, 'I think my father would be able to answer your question better, he is very friendly, you have nothing to be afraid of.'

Bob began to follow her down the tunnel of the cave and could see that the end of it was lit up by bright light. As he approached where the light was getting brighter, he was astonished at the sight before him. He saw a large collection of gigantic buildings like he'd never seen before, it was all strange to him. Suddenly he saw a craft that flew in the air and came and settled in front of him with a man sitting in it.

The man looked at him and said, 'Hello, please don't be afraid, I saw you come down the tunnel with Tarana and have come to take you to meet our father, I am Tarana's brother, Zanos.'

Bob nodded to him; he noticed that Tarana and Zanos had the same colour hair, which was very light and a pale yellow.

'Thank you, Zanos; I would love to meet your father,' Bob said as Tarana showed him how to get into the flying craft.

When all three of them were sitting comfortably, Zanos spoke into small section in front of him that seemed to bulge out a little from the edge of the front console. 'Take us to the Red Citadel.'

As the craft lifted and began to fly, Bob remembered about his trip with Vond in his spaceship. He looked all around him through the clear canopy and saw the city below, Bob was curious about where they were going, but didn't ask, he just enjoyed the ride and the view.

Soon they set down on a large landing that stuck out from one of the large high buildings. Bob was amazed at all the things he had seen. Tarana helped him out of the flying craft and led him to a door that opened by itself. It was all magical to him. Zanos didn't follow them, he stayed in flying craft.

Tarana took him to a place that was down a short tunnel as Bob saw it and then into another room where a man was standing near a large seat waiting for them. He looked at Bob and smiled.

'Hello there, my friend, I am Noorod, and I am Tarana's father. We haven't seen one of your people to talk to for a long time. Are you surprised to know there are other people living here on your world?'

Bob Nodded, 'Yes, no one is aware that such a place as your city exists, I only found it by accident and curiosity. How long have you been here?' Bob asked him, 'my name is Bob,' he added.

'We have been here for thousands of years, Bob, long before your people were as they are now.'

Bob was lost, 'What is, 'Thousands of years?'

Noorod realised that Bob's people would have no concept of years and months etc. 'Let's just say, Bob that we have been here for a very long time and come from another world in outer-space. We came and settled here when our own world was dying, we found Earth and stayed here.'

Bob then remembered about Vond telling him that he came from another world. 'Why have you never shown yourself to my people and other people that live here?' he asked Noorod.

'Because, Bob, we had enough to keep us occupied with building our city. It has taken many generation to come this far, and we didn't want to interfere with the progress of this planet's natural species.'

Bob didn't understand many of Noorod's words, but got the general idea of what he was saying.

'Will you ever come and see my people and others?' Bob asked him.

'Who knows, Bob, maybe one day, but the natural people of your world will need to progress a long way first. It would be wrong to interfere at such an early stage of your people's progress.'

'I cannot stay here very long; I am hunting for food for my people at the cave where I live. Do you understand that?' he asked Noorod.

'Yes, Bob, Tarana will take you back, but you can visit us any time you wish, but you must keep this place and our people secret from everyone else, will you do that?' Noorod asked him with concern.

'I promise I will tell no one about you, but I might come again sometime when I can spend more time here, if you are happy with that idea. I would like to see more of your city,' he said.

'Yes, Bob, that will be fine, you will be very welcome. Tarana will see you get back to the forest outside our cave entrance; I hope you have a good hunting day.'

Tarana, and her brother Zanos took Bob back to the cave entrance. Tarana then went back with Zanos. Bob waved goodbye to them and he set off back into the forest and was wondering what else he would find out about this world that he didn't know about under the

ground. He began to wonder if anyone else had seen such things as he had, but were telling no one about them. He was beginning to learn more about the world he was living in and finding there were all kinds of things to be found out that no one else knew about, this is another reason he liked to hunt by himself.

He was now moving through the forest and once again concentrating on hunting. He heard movement again in the grass and froze on the spot; he felt that it might be a large brown rabbit.

Looking around him he saw some grass move apart and two large brown rabbits came out from it and begin to eat some of the leaves of the plants. Bob slowly lifted his spear and took aim and then let it fly. His aim was good and he hit one of the large brown rabbits through its heart area and killed it almost right out. He threw his second one and hit it again; the second spear finished it off.

He went up to the rabbit and pulled his spears out of it. The rabbit was a really large

one, so he decided that he would head back home and be happy with this one and not go after the second. This one alone would make a good addition to his own family feast, but this time he didn't have any to share with the others.

He set off home feeling quite content with his day. He had made a few new friends, firstly with Skimpy the fox and then the people from the underground city, which he hoped to go back to some time.

He soon saw the outline of the caves in the distance and was ready to settle down and think about his days events. Bob knew that he couldn't tell his family about the underground city, but was still able to tell them he'd been in the thick forest and had had a good day's hunting.

Story 8

Bob and Siber Meet Mogar

It was a cold morning and Bob had got his thicker furs on. He knew that the winter snow would soon be falling and cover the land in a crisp white blanket.

Although it was cold, the sun was shining and the sky was clear and gave a good sign for a nice day.

As he walked along the northerly path, he saw Siber curled up in the long grass by the side of the pathway.

'Good morning, Bob,' Siber said with a smile, 'are you going far today?' he asked.

'I'm heading north; I'm hoping to meet up with my Homo-Sapien friend, Mogar. I haven't seen him for a while, the day I was going to

meet him, we had all that rain and the flooded pools stopped me from getting to him.'

Siber was keen to go with him, 'Can I come with you?' Siber asked remembering what Bob had promised him a few days earlier. He really hoped that Bob would agree and say yes.

Bob looked down at him a little unsure, 'If I say yes, do you promise to behave yourself?' Bob asked him with a firm voice, 'and do what I say if I tell you to do anything?'

Siber nodded his head, 'Yes, Bob, I promise to be good and not frighten any animals away you might want to kill. I really want to be your friend and go with you on your hunting days,' he told Bob.

'Alright, you can come, but if I tell you to stop and be quiet, you must do it straight away, do you understand,' Bob said in a firm voice.

'I understand, Bob, I will do what you say and do it straight away when you say,' Siber assured him.

'Alright, follow me by my side and don't get in front, or it might frighten animals away.'

They set off and followed the path. Bob was hoping to meet up with Mogar so he could arrange a meeting with Mogar's people and his own. Bob really wanted them to meet and become friendly with each other, he knew it would make a great difference to both peoples.

Siber was curious as to why Bob wanted his people to meet the Homo-Sapiens. 'Why do you want to meet your friend Mogar's people so much? They are different people to your own and have different ideas,' Siber asked.

Bob stopped and looked down at Siber who was slithering on his right side. 'Well, Siber, the main reasons are to become friendly with them and share our knowledge and different ideas. My father thinks it should help each of our peoples to grow stronger and grow together, maybe even live together at some stage,' he told him.

Siber gave him a thoughtful look, 'I think that will take some time to happen, Bob, there may be lots of ideas you don't agree with on both sides. It might cause conflict with all of you,' Siber said with sincere concern.

Bob pondered on what Siber had said and knew that Siber was genuinely concerned for him and Bob's own people, 'That might be true, Siber, but we can only find out by meeting and trying to get on together, I know there will be different ideas, but it's from those that we might make progress and move on to better things.'

'That's true, Bob, I just hope it all works out as you hope, it will be good if it all goes well,' Siber said.

'Well, Siber, we shall have to wait and see; only time will tell.'

As Bob looked ahead up the path they were following, he saw two rabbits in a patch of short grass. He realised they hadn't heard him and Siber talking.

Bob looked down at Siber as he took his sling from his hip and put one of his smooth stones in it ready to use, 'Siber, be quiet, there are two rabbits over there in a small clearing of short grass, I'm going to try and kill one of them, it will make a good start for the day's hunting,' he told him.

Siber nodded and lowered himself in the grass and Bob took aim with his sling at one of the rabbits. Bob swung his sling round his head and let his stone fly. It was a good shot and he hit one of the rabbits on the head and stunned it. It fell to the floor unconscious.

Bob quickly ran to the rabbit, he lifted it up by its hind legs and hit it behind its neck with the side of his hand and killed it.

Siber slithered up to him with a smile on his face. 'Well done, Bob, that was a good aim with your sling, you are very good with it, I'm still getting dizzy spells from you hitting me,' he said with a smile.

Bob smiled at him and said, 'Well, Siber, if you are good, I won't have to do it again, will I?' Bob said to him.

'No, Bob, I assure you I won't give you cause to hit me with a sling-stone again, once is enough,' he said still smiling, 'but the other rabbit has run away.'

Bob smiled back at him, 'That's not a problem, Siber, we might get a chance to get the another one on the way back, where there is one or two, there is usually more not far away,' he told Siber.

Bob fastened the rabbit to his hip with a piece of cord that he always carried with him for such occasions. They carried on along the path and hoped that they would soon meet Mogar.

As they moved down the path, Bob looked down at Siber, 'Siber, if we are lucky enough to meet my friend Mogar, I want you to lay low in the grass whilst I go and talk to him. I will need to tell him about you first before both of you meet. When he is aware of you, I will signal to

you and shout you over to us. That way, you won't frighten him and he won't attack you.

'Alright, Bob, I'll do as you say, I wouldn't want to make him jump or frighten him,' Siber said.

They continued up the path for a while and Bob saw someone in the distance walking towards them. As they got closer to each other, Bob saw that it was his Homo-Sapien friend, Mogar.

Soon they met and Siber waited a little further down the path in the long grass as Bob had told him to so Bob could speak with Mogar.

'Hello, Mogar, I'm so glad we have been able to meet again. I have good news, my father wants to meet your people to talk about sharing ideas and becoming friends with everyone,' Bob told him.

Mogar smiled with joy, 'That is good, Bob, my father who is second in charge to our chief, has spoken with our people and with me and

they are all eager to meet and share our ideas with your people, and other things too.'

Bob smiled at Mogar and was happy to hear his news, Bob then said, 'Mogar, I have a friend who I want you to meet, but please don't be frightened when you meet him, he won't harm you.'

Mogar was unsure what Bob meant as he couldn't see anyone with him. He looked around and saw no one. 'Who is this friend of yours, Bob? I don't see anyone with you,' Mogar asked him.

Bob smiled and looked behind him, 'Siber, it's alright for you to come out now and join us,' he said.

Siber slowly slithered out from the long grass and moved up to where Bob and Mogar were standing. Mogar couldn't speak to animals and other creatures like Bob could and wasn't sure how to react. Bob did the speaking for Siber and relayed it to Mogar; all Mogar could hear was Siber's hissing.

Siber told Bob to tell Mogar that he has nothing to be afraid of. Bob told Mogar what Siber had said and he felt a little easier, but was impressed that Bob could speak with such creatures and consider them friends.

Mogar looked down at Siber and said in a friendly voice, 'It's nice to meet you, Siber, I am Mogar.'

Siber hissed at Bob saying, 'Tell Mogar I am pleased to meet him.'

Bob told Mogar Siber's reply and Mogar just smiled at Siber and nodded.

Bob had an idea, 'Mogar shall we see what we can catch between us and share what we kill?' he asked him.

'That's a good idea, Bob, let's see what is around, I saw signs of some more Warthogs on my way here, it would be good if we could kill one each again like before,' Mogar suggested.

'That sounds a good to me, Mogar, let's go and see if we can find them.'

They set of in the direction that Mogar had come to see if they could find any definite signs of the Warthogs. Siber followed behind them and ready to help in any way he could. Siber was quite excited at being with Bob and his new friend, Mogar.

Bob and Mogar walked slowly and quietly looking and listening for any signs of Warthogs, or anything they could kill.

As they walked down the grassy path, they came to a spot where they saw some tracks of Warthogs passing across the path going to their right. They turned and began to follow the tracks and hoped they would find them.

There were tracks suggesting that there were four Warthogs probably looking for food.

Very soon the tracks led them to where three warthogs were forging under the grassy forest floor for grubs and other food they ate. Bob wondered where the fourth Warthog could be and saw no signs of it.

They crept up behind some bushes so the Warthogs wouldn't see them and made ready with their throwing spears.

Bob whispered to Mogar, 'You aim at the one on the left and I'll aim at the one on the right. The third one will probably run away.'

Bob and Mogar took aim with their spears whilst Siber settled down in the grass and looked at the Warthogs whilst peeping above the tall grass.

Bob and Mogar let fly with their spears and both spears hit the Warthogs they were aiming at. The third one as expected ran away into the long grass leaving his two friends dying and screaming out in pain as they fell over onto their sides. Both spears had hit vital organs and had nearly killed the Warthogs. Bob and Mogar ran over to them and speared them again through their hearts and killed them. The two Warthogs went silent.

As they were pulling their spears out from the two dead Warthogs, They suddenly saw the

fourth one charging at them from the long grass and taking no notice of their spears.

Siber quickly reacted and moved into action and slithered in between Bob and Mogar and the Warthog. He rose up and hissed loudly at the Warthog. The Warthog came to a skidding stop with his front paws in the leaf covered ground. Siber struck with his fangs, but the Warthog was too quick for him and turned on his heels and ran off into the grass and bushes.

Bob and Mogar were amazed and impressed at Siber's bravery and speed and knew that he had saved them from possible injury from the charging creature.

'Well done, Siber,' Bob shouted over to him.

'Yes, Siber, thank you for helping stop the Warthog's attack, we could have been badly hurt by it if it had have reached us,' Mogar added.

Siber nodded and smiled in his snake-ish way and understood what Mogar had said.

Bob and Mogar knew that Siber understood Mogar.

Siber looked at Bob and said, 'Tell, Mogar that it was the only thing to do when I saw the Warthog charging from the bushes. I didn't want any of you getting hurt by it.'

Bob told Mogar what Siber had said and Mogar looked and smiled at Siber and said, 'Thank you, Siber.'

As before, Bob and Mogar cut some of the meat from each animal and Bob made a fire and soon they were roasting the meat ready to eat.

They ate and chatted and Bob threw Siber some of the raw meat for him to eat. Siber didn't like cooked meat, he was used to killing small creatures like mice and rats and ate them whole and slowly digested them over several days.

Bob looked across to Mogar, 'I'm looking forward to our people meeting each other, Mogar, it will be interesting to see how things go,' he said.

'Yes, I too, Bob, I hope it all works out, I think we shall learn new things from each other. Even if it doesn't work out, we can still be friends, but I feel everyone will mix very easily,' Mogar assured Bob.

Bob was curious, 'Mogar, do your people live in caves?' he asked him.

Mogar smiled, 'Well, we used to, but now we live in our own made huts that we make from straw, grass, mud and branches from trees. We use caves for storing food for winter and other times of need. We have lived like this for many generations,' Mogar told him then asked, 'Do you still live in Caves?'

'We live in three different caves that are close together and in a long stretch of cliffs. The cliffs are in a valley and the caves are in the higher part that helps keep water from getting

into them. We don't live in huts like you, that is something we can learn from you,' Bob explained to him.

Siber was listening to them talking and asked Bob, 'Bob, do you think your people would accept me being your friend, even though I am a snake?'

Bob smiled at him and said, 'I don't think so, Siber, my people don't know I can speak to animals and certain other creatures, and I don't think they would feel comfortable with a snake hanging around, no matter how friendly you are.'

'That is a shame, I would have loved to see what happens in your caves and join in what you all do. But at least I have two friends, you and Mogar.'

Bob explained to Mogar what Siber had said and turned back to Siber and said, 'I suggest you find a high point near our caves and observe from there, that's about the nearest you'll get

without being seen. If anyone sees you, they are sure to attack you.'

Siber looked at him a little disappointed, 'Alright, Bob, I understand what you are saying. I'll do what you say and be sure to keep out of sight.'

Mogar couldn't understand what Siber was saying, but was impressed how Bob spoke to him and wished he could do the same.

Soon they had finished eating and that it was time for both of them to make a travois so they could take their warthog home to each of their peoples.

Siber couldn't do anything to help, so he kept a lookout for any possible dangers.

It didn't take them long to make their travois' and loaded the Warthogs on them ready to pull home.

Bob and Mogar said their goodbyes and set off to their own homes. Siber smiled at Mogar

and nodded to him. Mogar took this as a goodbye and smiled back at him.

They were soon out of sight of each other as Siber slithered by Bob's right side.

'I think it's a good idea for each your people to meet each other, Bob. You will advance and learn each other many things, maybe even live together one day,' he said.

'Yes, Siber, that's what I'm hoping for, maybe I might find a mate that lives with Mogar's people.'

As they walked through the bushes and high grasses, Bob suddenly heard something heading in their direction. Bob ducked down in the grass and Siber lay by him trying to peep over the grass to see if he could see anything.

Suddenly, Bob saw a black and white creature coming through the grass. Bob recognized who it was and sighed with relief, for a moment he thought it could be a lion or hyena.

He stood up and saw that it was Cob, the badger who he knew very well. 'Hello, Cob, I'm surprised to see you, you are a good distance from your Set.'

Cob looked at Bob, 'The hunting isn't too good near our set at the moment, so I am exploring a little further out,' he told him.

'Don't you think it's a little dangerous in the daylight, Cob? You normally hunt at night.'

'Yes, Bob, but my mate has just had four babies and we need extra food. Don't worry; Bob, I'll be alright,' he said and then added, 'it looks like you have had a good day.'

'Yes, Cob, you are welcome to have some if you wish, it's a large Warthog.'

Cob smiled back at him, 'Thank you for your offer, Bob, but we don't like that kind of meat, it's a bit rich for us, we prefer smaller things like bugs or mice or even worms, but thanks for asking,' Cob said.

'Well, Cob, it's getting late, we'll be off and let you get going, good luck and be careful,' Bob said.

'I will, don't worry about me, I will be fine,' Cob said and carried on his way.

Bob and Siber carried on and eventually Siber went off on his own to rest for the night after his exciting day with Bob and Mogar.

'Bye, Siber, I'll see you again in a few days. I will be going with my people on the winter hunt tomorrow for a few days; I'll see you when we get back.'

'Very well, Bob, I hope you have a good hunt,' he said then disappeared in the long grass.

Bob set off home and was soon nearing the caves he could see in the distance. He was keen to tell his father about meeting Mogar and what he had said and that Mogar's people were agreeable to meet up with them after the winter hunt to discuss their future.

Story 9

Neanderthal Bob and the Winter Hunt

All the male hunters of the three caves were gathered around a central camp fire, the three chiefs were sat together, Blowen, Bob's father, Too-gart, chief of the second cave and Koop, the chief of the first cave.

Bob was sitting next to his father to his right with the other two chiefs to his father's left. Bob's father stood up and addressed everyone around the central fire.

Well everyone, this is the first of two main hunts before the heavy winter snows come. Those who go with me will be travelling North-west, the second group will be going North-east. Each will get to the migration routes of the herds travelling south for the winter. If each group can get at least four good sized animals each, it will

be a good start for our food to last us over the winter. On our second hunt, we will hopefully get the same amount again that will see us through the whole winter with what we catch on the first hunt. Bob will be coming with me and half of the hunters and Too-gart and Koop will be leading the second group. Are there any questions?' he asked them.

One of the hunters, Duni asked, 'Are we taking our mates with us as usual to help cut up the meat and smoke it?'

He looked at Duni, 'Yes, Duni, we will be taking our mates as usual, some of the hunters will be staying behind to watch over the caves with the women and children that are not going with us.'

Duni nodded accepting Blowen's words. The hunters that were staying behind were not at the hunting meeting, they were making preparations so that the entire valley was secure to keep out wild animals. This was done by a series of fences around the outer areas.

Blowen told the hunters who were going with each group to be ready to set off early the following morning. The hunters' mates who were going were leaving any children they had with the other women who were not going.

When all the hunters had gone back to their mates and caves, Bob asked his father a question about the meeting with the Homo-Sapiens.

'Father, I have arranged to meet Mogar in a few days after the hunt, we will then arrange a day for you and some of our people to go and meet his people; is that alright with you?'

Blowen smiled at Bob, 'Yes, Bob, that will be good, we are looking forward to meeting his people and Mogar as well. It will be a day to remember, I just hope everything works out for our people and theirs.'

Bob nodded to his father, 'I'm sure it will everyone seems to be looking forward to meeting Mogar's people.'

'We can only wait and see, Bob,' Blowen told him.

* * *

The following morning, all the hunters were gathered outside Blowen's cave ready to set off on their two hunting expeditions. Bob was ready with his three spears and sling together with his magical foraging stick.

Koop and Too-gart set off first to the North-east and were hopeful of a good trip. Blowen gathered his group together including the women and said, 'We are travelling to the North-West. We will walk with two rows of hunters in line with the women in the middle for protection reasons. Any signs of danger, shout out loud so we can deal with it quickly. We are all familiar with the direction we are going in, but keep alert at all times for potential kills,' he told them.

They set off with Bob walking opposite Blowen at the front and his mother between them.

The morning was damp and misty, but showed signs of brightening up in the distance. To get to the migration fields would take most of the day and they chatted between themselves as they walked, but keeping aware of the areas around them for any possible targets to kill or potential attacks from the wild predators.

It was about mid morning when a shout came from the rear of the lines, 'HYENAS!'

All the hunters turned and ran to where the shout came from; it was a young hunter who had shouted the alarm. As the hunters gathered in a ready position, they saw six hyenas about thirty body lengths to their east side. They watched the hyenas and were ready to attack them if need be.

In Blowen's group there were twenty hunters in all and all very good shots with their slings.

Blowen shouted, Get ready with your slings, we will aim a full volley at them to try and scare them off.'

All the hunters made ready with their slings and began to wave them round in the air ready to let them fly in the direction of the hyenas.

'Now!' shouted Blowen and all stones flew at the hyenas. Some of them hit them as screams of pain were heard by the hunters.

The hyenas began to back away and two of them actually ran off leaving the others alone.

Blowen shouted, 'Do the same again and aim to hit them where it hurts them most!" he shouted to them again.

Once more the hunters aimed their slings at the remaining hyenas and all stones hit the animals and caused them pain. The remaining hyenas began to run off following the first two.

Blowen and the hunters watched as they disappeared into the distant trees and were soon out of sight.

'Well done everyone, I think we scared them off in no uncertain terms. Hopefully we won't see them again on this hunt.'

Bob added, 'Hyena meat is very tough anyway; it would be a last resort to eat their meat.'

Blowen smiled at him, 'Yes, Bob, you're right,' Blowen looked at the other hunters, 'Let's get back to where we were and carry on.'

They all went back to their original position in the lines and carried on. The women had all crouched down in the long grass whilst the hunters were warding off the hyenas and were now getting back in line as before.

The day went well and everyone was getting ready to reach the migration fields and to set up camp and make ready for the following day's hunt. It wasn't long before they were approaching their destination.

Bob lifted his arm and pointed, 'Father, look, there is a herd of deer grazing, I think we should make camp here and then make our attack early in the morning before the herd moves on.'

'Good idea, Bob.'

Blowen turned and said quietly to the others, 'We will make camp here, get everything ready for smoking and cutting up the meet when we kill the deer tomorrow. We need to make six fires around the boundary to ward of any predators; you all know the system so let's get everything done,' he told everyone.

Soon everything was ready and camp fires were made on the inner part also for them to sit and sleep around. Plenty of firewood was collected to keep the fires burning and everyone settled down for the night.

Bob was thinking about Mogar, 'Father, how many do you think we should take to meet Mogar's party of people?'

I think about a quarter of ours mixed with men women and one or two children. I would guess that Mogar's people will bring a mixture of theirs too.'

'That sounds good, I am looking forward to us meeting them, we should do well if we can work or even live together,' Bob said.

'I am curious to see what we can learn from them and them from us,' Bob's mother said.

'Do they live in caves like we do, Bob?' Blowen asked him.

'No Father, they live in what Mogar calls huts that are made from grass, twigs and branches from trees covered in grass and mud from the rivers. He said that they would teach us how to build them. However, they use nearby caves to store their food and other things they have.'

Blowen nodded, 'It all sounds very interesting, I like the idea of the huts you speak of, I think we will learn a great deal from them,' he said.

'How do they hunt, Bob?' his mother asked him.

'From what I have learnt from Mogar, they hunt in the same way as we do, and use the same type of weapons, but Mogar's spears are better made and are straighter. He told me he was going to teach me how they got them so straight. He said something about using fire and water.'

Muna, his mother nodded and said, 'They are more advanced than we are, but I feel we have ideas to offer them too.'

'We will soon find out, Mother, we are all keen to meet them.'

Soon everyone was ready for settling down and two hunters stood guard and were relieved by two more hunters later. The change of guards was done about four times through the night.

The night went well and they had no visits from any predators. Everyone was aware of night predators and the guards were very alert to any danger.

* * *

The following morning, everyone was up at the crack of dawn and the men were ready to go and make their kills. Bob took a group, Blowen took a group and two other experienced hunters took two more groups. The idea was for each group to position themselves so they could all get a deer each, making four kills.

The herd of deer were scattered quite widely which was good for the hunters, it meant they could attack at the same time and hopefully make their kills easily.

They all set off and found their best spot ready to throw their spears at their targets. Blowen was able to see the four hunter groups and would wave his arm downwards when ready to make their move.

The herd was not expecting the hunters and Blowen lifted his arm ready to give the signal. Moments later he dropped it and all the hunter ran at their targets and let their spears fly.

Three of the groups were successful and each spear from each group hit their target. The

fourth group were unlucky as the deer they were attacking herd them and ran off at speed; this caused the rest of the herd to take flight and was soon out of sight on their migration south.

They all went to their kill and the fourth group joined them to help move each deer to the camp for cutting up and smoking.

They divided into three groups and pulled each of the deer to their camp. The women were ready and immediately began to cut the deer up and to smoke it over specially prepared smoker fires. They had three in all and soon had the deer meat smoking over the frames to preserve the meet. The men were making several travois' for pulling the meat back to the caves.

Blowen was well please with their kills, even though they didn't get a fourth one, but the deer were quite large and compensated for not getting the four they set out to get.

The preparing and smoking took most of the day, but by the time the evening came, all the meat was smoking well and would be ready for

the following day to go back to their caves. The hunters on guard would keep the fires going and make sure the smoker fires were furbished with the right leaves to keep them smoking the meat.

Bob had just been woken up to take the second watch with Scuna, one of the other hunters. The night had so far been quiet and it was a beautiful star-lit night and the moon was shining bright.

Bob looked up at the moon and remembered his trip with Vond; he knew that none of his people would believe his story so just smiled to himself thinking about what he saw on the moon.

Scuna saw him looking up at the moon, 'Do you think our ancestors are looking down upon us, Bob?' Scuna asked.

Bob looked at him and smiled, 'I'm sure they are, Scuna, but I think there is more to the second great light in the sky than we know about.'

Scuna thought Bob's answer was a bit strange, 'What makes you say that, Bob?'

Bob smiled, 'Well, Scuna, I think that what we see in the night sky is one big mystery and that some of the tiny dots we see lighting up the blackness are possibly worlds like ours, and maybe some might have people living on them like our world,' he told Scuna.

Scuna was amazed at what Bob had said as he had never heard anyone say anything like that before. 'Those are strange words, Bob, but I suppose you could be right.'

'We will never know, Scuna.'

Moments later, Scuna said, 'Bob, I've just heard something over there near the smoking fires. We have an unwanted visitor.'

They quickly woke everyone up, even the women. Blowen jumped to his feet and went over to Bob and Scuna. Bob pointed to where the noise had been heard.

Scuna, Bob and Blowen took their spears and walked over to the area where the noise had been heard, the rest of the hunters were ready with their spears in case anything attacked. The women moved away from the noise and got behind the large central fires.

As Bob, Scuna and Blowen got nearer the spot, they saw two wolves sneaking in the grass.

Blowen quietly said to the hunters, 'When I say "Now", aim your spears.' Moments later Blown said, 'Now!'

Each threw their spears and other hunters threw their spears as well. Two loud screams came from the fatally wounded wolves. Each wolf had at least three spears in them from the other hunters as well as Bob's, Blowen's and Scuna's.

The wolves soon gave up the ghost and lay dead. Blowen looked down at them and said, 'Well done, Scuna, I think they were after our meat from the kills, but they could have attacked us too. We will take them with us; wolf meat is

quite good, although a little tough, its fair game for eating.'

Some of the women came and took the wolves and gutted them and prepared them so they could be carried hanging on two poles by two hunters.

Everyone eventually settled down to sleep for what was left of the night. The excitement had stirred them all up, but thankfully no one was hurt.

* * *

The morning soon came and everyone was up and ready to set off back to the caves. Spirits were high. Although they hadn't killed four deer, the wolves would compensate the loss of the fourth and with the extra large deer too.

Four of the hunters carried the dead wolves on the poles and the rest pulled the smoked meat from the deer on the travois'. Some of the women pulled the travois' too as the meat was quite extensive. The hunt had been good and

would make a good start for the winter food store.

It was approaching evening when they reached the caves and everyone was happy to see them back safe. The second hunting party had had a great hunt and had killed two deer and two aurochs. This was going to make a large store of meat. The two wolves were skinned cut up and shared between the three caves and were eaten as part of the evening meals. On the way home, the women who were not pulling travois' were able to collect a good amount of wild vegetables and herbs.

The hunt was a great success; they would now have to plan the second hunt, which would be in a few days time after the meeting with Mogar's people.

Everyone went to sleep that night with a full stomach and very contented.

Printed in Great Britain
by Amazon

11309156R00061